S0-BCW-199

Just Right

Written by Melissa Schiller
Illustrated by Elliot Kreloff

SCHOLASTIC INC.

New York Toronto London Auckland Sydney
Mexico City New Delhi Hong Kong Buenos Aires

Copyright © 2000 by Scholastic Inc. All rights reserved. Published by Scholastic Inc. Portions previously published in SCHOLASTIC DECODABLE READERS. SCHOLASTIC, SCHOLASTIC PHONICS READY READERS, and associated logos are trademarks and/or registered trademarks of Scholastic Inc.

12 11 10 9 8 7 6 5   4 5 6 7/0

Printed in the U.S.A.   08

Sam and Dad play with blocks. Sam sets blocks right on top. Soon Sam's block tower is really high! Sam needs Dad's help. So Dad lifts Sam up.

Sam and Dad sit on the grass. Sam
sees an owl fly by. It goes in its nest way
up high in the tree. Sam waves at it.

Sam and Dad are at the beach. The sun shines bright.

Sam and Dad jump in the waves and kick and splash. Dad finds a seashell and holds it up to Sam's ear. It sounds just like the waves.

Sam and Dad visit the park. They play
ball. Dad helps Sam hold his bat just right.

Then Sam hits the ball up, up, up, and
out of sight!

Now Sam and Dad eat hot dogs and
drink milk for lunch. Sam thinks hot dogs
and milk are the best!

When they finish, Sam helps Dad clean
up. They make a good team.

That night, Sam and Dad read. Sam hugs Dad while Dad holds Sam tight. Then Sam sees a falling star!

Sam makes a wish. He wishes he'll grow up to be just like Dad.

Vowel /ī/ *igh, y*

bright
by
fly
high
night
right
sight
tight